Ladybird

This Little Story

belongs to

_____

Published by Ladybird Books Ltd
80 Strand London WC2R 0RL
A Penguin Company

17 19 20 18 16

Printed in Italy

Little
Blue Tractor

by Nicola Baxter
illustrated by Toni Goffe

Farmer Fred scratched his head.

"It's going to snow and it's going to blow," he said, "or I'm a turnip. All the animals *must* come into the barn."

So the Little Blue Tractor and his trailer trundled off across the farm to find the pigs.

How does he know it's going to snow?

The pigs were in the pen, snuffling and munching.

"You must come into the barn," said the Little Blue Tractor. "Farmer Fred *thinks* it's going to snow."

"Snow?" grunted the greedy pigs. "How does he know it's going to snow? We're staying right here... *snuffle*... with these... *munch*... tasty turnip tops, thank you very much."

So off trundled the Little Blue Tractor to find the cows.

How does he know it's going to snow?

The cows were in the meadow, chewing and mooing.

"You must come into the barn," said the Little Blue Tractor. "Farmer Fred *says* it's going to snow."

"*Ooo*h, n*ooo*," the cows mooed slowly. "A little bit of sn*ooo*w doesn't worry us, you kn*ooo*w. We're not… *chew*… leaving this… *chew*… ju*uuu*icy green grass, thank you very much."

So off trundled the Little Blue Tractor to find the hens.

The hens were in the yard, pecking and scratching.

"You must come into the barn," said the Little Blue Tractor. "Farmer Fred is *sure* it's going to snow."

"Snow? What's that?" clucked the hens nervously. "Now we're all of a twitter. Don't come bothering us... *cluck*... with silly... *cluck*... stories, thank you very much."

So off trundled the Little Blue Tractor to find the ducks.

The ducks were on the pond, dipping and diving.

"You must come into the barn," said the Little Blue Tractor. "Farmer Fred is *certain* it's going to snow."

"Is that a fact?" quacked the dabbling ducks. "We're not worried by a little bit of wind and wet. We're… *quack*… happy… *quack*… whatever the weather, thank you very much."

So off trundled the Little Blue Tractor to find the sheep.

quack

The sheep were on the hillside, huddled together.

"You must come into the barn," said the Little Blue Tractor. "Farmer Fred *knows* it's going to snow."

"The b*aaa*rn?" bleated the sheep. "You must be b*aaa*rmy, our woolly coats are the warmest on the f*aaa*rm, thank you very much."

So off trundled the Little Blue Tractor to find the horse.

The horse was in the paddock, lazily leaning on the gate.

"You must come into the barn," said the Little Blue Tractor. "Farmer Fred is *as sure as he can be* that it's going to snow."

"Tod*aaa*y?" neighed the horse with a yawn. "Oh, what a bore. I'd rather st*aaa*y, old chap, thank you very much."

So off trundled the Little Blue Tractor back to the farmhouse.

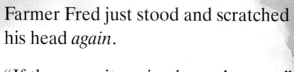

Farmer Fred just stood and scratched his head *again*.

"If those uppity animals won't come," he said, "they can stay where they are. *You* can go into the barn."

And he went back into the warm farmhouse and banged the door shut.

As the Little Blue Tractor trundled across the yard, the first fluffy flakes of snow began to fall.

The Little Blue Tractor looked out from the barn. On the farm everything was white and whirling.

"It's snowing and blowing all right," he thought. "Oh bother! I can't stay here. I'm going to have to bring those uppity animals into the barn."

So off trundled the Little Blue Tractor. The snow was cold and crunchy and an icy wind whistled round his wheels.

Bother those uppity animals!

The Little Blue Tractor came to the pig pen. "Come on pigs, you can bring those turnip tops with you," he said. And the pigs climbed into the trailer without a grunt or a grumble.

The Little Blue Tractor came to the meadow. "Come on cows," he said, "your grass isn't green now!" And the cows climbed into the trailer without a moo or a moan.

The Little Blue Tractor came to the yard. "Come on hens," he said, "before your beaks turn blue." And the hens fluttered on board without a twitter or a cluck.

The Little Blue Tractor came to the pond. It was frozen solid. "Come on you daft ducks," he said. And the ducks slid across the ice without a single quack.

The Little Blue Tractor came to the hillside. Even the sheep were shivering. "Come on, there's room for all of you," said the Little Blue Tractor kindly. And they shuffled on board without a baa or a bleat.

The Little Blue Tractor came to the paddock. "Come on horse, follow us!" he cried. And the horse lolloped quietly behind him all the way back to the barn.

All night long it was snowing and blowing. But the Little Blue Tractor and the pigs and the cows and the hens and the ducks and the sheep and the horse were safe in the barn.

And with a grunt and a moo and a cluck and a quack and a baa and a neigh, all those uppity animals turned to say, "Little Blue Tractor, *thank you very much!*"

It was nothing. Really.